MYSTERIES OF THE MAGIC WELL

A Quest to find Adam Smith

A book by

Netanya D' Costa

Clever Fox
PUBLISHING

Chennai • Bangalore

CLEVER FOX PUBLISHING
Chennai, India

Published by CLEVER FOX PUBLISHING 2023
Copyright © Netanya D' Costa 2023

AUTHOR'S NOTE

My name is Netanya D'Costa and I study in grade six (VI). Although I wrote this book almost a year ago, it has been hard to edit or find a good publisher and study at the same time (pandemic confinement!). One of the most inspiring reasons to write this book was my grand-father (nanu: Maj Gen Krishan Chauhan, who is also an author). After mentioning my grandfather, I certainly can't forget my beloved nani; Reeta Chauhan who was the driving force of both me and my grandfather to write these books (and lots of other stuff!) Ever since the age of nine, I have written poems and short stories. I wrote most of this book during the covid-19 pandemic and it served as a way to escape to a fictional world away from all the madness. Other than writing I also enjoy being an orator (Am most definitely called a chatter-box), love beaches: therefore swimming, basketball, mathematics and building things.

My mother Anisha D'Costa has always told me that Expectations = Disappointments, which is why I don't expect for my book to be published, but I hope so. My mother has urged me to finish, edit, summarize and write this book. She was one of the biggest help for this book to be a success. She is also the designer of this book's cover-page. My father(mon pere, French) was a huge help in reading and editing this book (Proof-reader). I am very thankful for his help. I also thank my sister (can't call her trash here right? P.S Sibling Love,sic!) for encouraging me and making improvements to my work (If I was motivating her I would just say, "always remember :" It is trash can- not trash cannot").

CONTENTS

CHAPTER 1

A GAME OF HIDE AND SEEK

Once upon a time, in a deep enchanted forest there was a well. Not any well, a magic well full of wonders and dreams. This well was in the northern forest and it was said that not one soul had ever been known to see it. Alas, the well was found and now is known to only a few people alive. Near the forest was a town; quite a lovely place, really a beach in the southwest and forests up north. Its name is **Magicae Oppidum (which in Latin means magic town)**, a town where Sue, James, Kyra and Peter lived. One fine and sunny day of their summer holidays and James's tenth birthday, Kyra and James were getting ready to go for a party in the woods. Since they had food with them and the forest was not too far, they decided to go on their bikes.

"Kyra, my bike has a punctureand I can't go on foot. How will I get there?" James whined but in the end, he rode on the back of Kyra's bike (although he thought it was not very grown up to ride on your sister's bike).

Meanwhile, Peter asked his mother if he could go out to meet his friends for a small party in the woods. His mother replied, "Do take some lemonade and something like sandwiches to eat. Convey my birthday wishes to James and beware of animals. Don't do anything reckless, oh ! why do I even bother, of course, you'll do something reckless! Just go and don't play in the sun too much, it's hot outside. Have fun!"

Peter agreed gave a cheeky grin and set off towards the forest.

Meanwhile, in the forest Kyra, her little brother James and Kyra's best friend Sue were waiting for Peter. Sue was the oldest in the group of friends being twelve. Peter and Kyra missed being the oldest and were younger by a few months. James was the youngest at ten years old, he always felt that because of which he was treated like a baby (or so he says, I say that he was like a king!) and often said, "I'm not small! It's not my fault that mum decided to have Kyra first!". Kyra was of average height, brown-eyed, the silent type who liked to keep her thoughts to herself and was a great student whereas her brother James had dark hair with the same intelligent eyes but instead of being quiet like Kyra, he loved to talk and hated when she told him to be quiet. Peter was always late unlike the others and he was always losing things. Sometimes it was his backpack or maybe even the whole picnic basket. He and Sue had blond hair and Peter had blue eyes much like Sue's grey ones. Because of this most people mistook them for siblings which drove Sue crazy as apart from hair and eyes they were quite different. For example, Sue had a great jawline but Peter's was average. Sue's hair was wavy while Peter's was short and straight.

Peter loved to tinker, and his room was like a mini workshop . No one understood his passion for these little treasures which he had tucked away in his room. Finally, Sue had a dog, Taffy, a German Shepard and Border Collie mix. Her mother was a very beautiful Collie named Pixy that Sue's mother found deserted in a field when she was giving birth. Sue was seven years of age at that time and begged her mom to let her keep Taffy, the name she had given to the pup. Her mother, a kindhearted soul, agreed and ever since Taffy has lived with them. She almost always went with the children when they were in the woods and could do several fun tricks. Taffy's mother too lived with them, but she was old and rarely went with the children and kept near Sue's mom.

"Oh, finally he came!" exclaime James in an overly dramatic voice while seeing a tired Peter running towards them. Peter's face was red, and he was panting because he ran all the way from home. "Hello everyone, I'm here!" he said between breaths.

"Hello, Peter. It sure is hot today, I'm melting like an icecream!" Sue said. Lucky for the children, Peter's mother made the best lemonade, not too sweet not too sour and with loads of ice. They all sang happy birthday to James (who acted all modest but inside he obviously loved it), went to town, had cake and played with Taffy trying to teach her how to roll over and speak. After a small picnic of salad, sandwiches and lots of cookies, James suggested they play hide and seek as a party game as it was not so hot anymore.

"Ok, let's race. The person who reaches the finish line last will be the seeker!" Sue said. Obviously, she was the second fastest after Peter and would not lose (cheater!). They all ran till the end, Kyra finished last, so she started counting, 1, 2, 3, 4, 5, 6 all the way till a hundred and ten (ten more seconds because she talked really quick).

Sue, the most acrobatic of the lot, climbed a tree and disguised herself among the branches (I guess it was a good day to wear green). Peter, who was the worst at hide and seek, climbed into a bush and immediately regretted it as there were thorns and now, he was stuck, ugh! He thought to himself, not again! (yes, dear reader, it has happened before many, many times). James ran and caught sight of a well. "Yes," he thought. "I'll get in the bucket, and they'll never find me!" He climbed into the bucket and it was as if the bucket was made for him, he fitted perfectly (but while he was there he wondered why is there a well so far from the town and that he had never seen or heard of wells in this area).

After what seemed to him a few minutes of pondering he heard his friends shouting. "James! James! Where are you? The game is over, it's been an hour! Come out," and other things he did not quite understand. James got out of the bucket and ran toward them at full speed but when they saw him, all of them gave a small yelp like someone had poked them with a needle. Sue said with her voice trembling, "James, what happened?"

CHAPTER 2

HOW TO BREAK A SPELL

When he came nearer, Kyra told James to investigate the well. James was shocked to see his reflection in the well. He had pointy ears, whiskers and a tail, but his body structure was one of a human! He also constantly mewed.

"Oh, no. I… meow…. look terrible. What…. meow happened?... meow. Why do I look like…. meow…. this? Why are you saying it's been an…. meow…. hour? I can't even…. meow…. Speak…. Meow…. properly!" Wailed James with his eyes flooding with tears. Kyra consoled her brother.

"Where have you been? It's been hours, we were all looking for you. What happened? Do you know what your mother would do if Kyra went home without you?" Sue exclaimed looking both angry and concerned (yes, I don't know how to do that either).

James told them how it was only for a few minutes he was in the well.

During all this, Peter was stuck in the bush, trying to get out while Kyra was with James. Clearly, Peter had to think his hiding spots through, Sue heard him and went through the rather painful job of pulling him out. "Ouch! Watch it, Sue! I have thorns all over my back!" he said.

"Not just your back, they're everywhere!" Sue replied (she now decided that one more whine and she would throw him back into the bushes).

While no one was looking, a series of words appeared on the flat rock in front of the old well. It read, **'If you wish to turn back, go and visit Ms. Clair Mac! She will tell you about me and thy shall find something in the tree'.** The children looked puzzled.

"Which tree and who is this Ms. Clair Mac and what just happened?" James asked Sue that he was having a bad dream, nope it was a nightmare.

Sue gave a sudden smile, "I know who she is, one of my mother's regular customers at the boutique. She lives at house number 472, Oak Street. Maybe if we go there, James will turn back! Come on, I'll lead the way. Follow me," the children trooped toward Ms. Clair Mac's house while Peter pulled the thorns out of his clothes.

" Hey! Pete bet you regret your hiding spot now! Even when I told you mine was better! Bahahaha," Sue teased when she saw him. Peter rolled his eyes and said that surely, he would win next time. When they reached the house of Ms.Clair Macthey saw a small black wooden cottage with a big garden and an enormous willow tree at the fence. They looked around and found her crying in the garden saying poor Fuzzy repeatedly. "Umm… excuse me. Hi, are you Ms. Clair Mac?" Sue asked politely.

The woman wiped her eyes and softly said, "Yes, hello Sue. I am Ms. Clair Mac. How may I help you and your friends?"

Sue replied, "We were wondering if you knew about a well in the forest."

She looked at the children, "Oh! Good heavens, no! I've never seen it, but there is an old story that tells you about a magic well in the forest."

Sue then persuaded her to tell them the story of the well.

She gave in and said, "Once upon a time, there was a well near our town. The people said that it belonged to a good witch who was defeated by an evil one for control over the well as it was a powerful item of magic. But both lost the battle.

When the good witch knew that she could not defeat the evil witch, the good witch put her magic into the well. She told her husband to put the only object that could kill the witch, in a safe place and lock it. He should then give the key to her child and send the child far away so she will be safe. Decades after the war, the evil witch won.

Some people believe that she killed the good witch. Others think the good witch escaped to a different land because sheknew that when her child was of age, she would kill the evil witch. So, the well can be controlled by anyone now. But it's just a story, I wonder why you are interested in it anyway!"

The children exchanged knowing glances among themselves. Ms. Clair asked, "Sue how is your mother? I would very much like to visit her sometime!"

Sue replied, "She is fine, Ms. Clair. You must visit her sometime!"

Then Peter quickly cut her off. "Miss, do you happen to know how a spell from the well can be broken once put on someone? You know, just out of curiosity." Peter asked curiously, dying to know how. The children were so eager to know that the whole world seemed to be in slow motion. Kyra was even sweating hard. Ms. Clair Mac thought for quite some time (it seemed as though she thought about the answer for an hour, but that is totally untrue!) and then finally replied, "It is said that a spell can be broken if you help someone in need as it uses the good witch's magic. Anyway, I doubt anyone will ever really find it because it's not real children, it's just an old story!"

But, boy, someone did find it!

CHAPTER 3

A DISCOVERY

"Aha! Now I know what to do," Peter thought to himself. It appears the others understood his thoughts for their expressions were exactly the same.

"Miss, why were you crying when we saw you earlier?" Kyra asked, recalling seeing her crying when they first came in and that they were supposed to do something with a tree.

"That's so sweet of you to ask, my dear girl. What was your name again? Pardon me, I'm quite forgetful. Well, you see, my cat Fuzzy is lost in that willow tree and I'm afraid it's rather large and I cannot climb anymore," said Ms. Clair.

"We could help you find her, miss," Sue replied. "What a wonderful thought, thank you, my dears. You don't know how much Fuzzy means to me. He is my best friend and companion!" Ms. Clair said to the children with tears of joy that she was being helped.

After hours of searching, Peter climbed down for a sip ofwater, Sue was stuck and was trying to get down and even Kyra gave up but just as she was climbing down, she caught sight of Fuzzy in the hollow of the tree, under Fuzzy was a small dark object, she could make out the figure of a book and chest. She quickly and quietly put it in her pocket and proceeded to go down the tree with Fuzzy. She nearly slipped halfway and then at the last branch, Fuzzy bit her. She fell into the flower bed and crushed the poppies there. Taffy immediately started barking and Fuzzy fluffed up like a tree, Sue had to call off Taffy though. When Kyra and Fuzzy got up, Ms. Clair gave her an enormous hug and said, "Thank you so much, Kyra." She hugged Fuzzy, put her inside, gave the children a hug each and bid them farewell after giving them a treat of some chocolates and tea.

They left Ms. Clair's house happily and went back to James who was hiding behind a rose bush, he had transformed back to his normal self with a huge amount of light glitter and clouds. "Yay! I'm finally myself! I was getting so tired of mewing. Thanks, guys. That rosebush is big. Oh, look, my tail's gone!" James said to the others, grinning.

"I liked cat James, though it looked cute," Sue said laughing and gave him his chocolate.

Kyra showed everyone the chest and the book, she said, "Hey guys, I found this under Fuzzy in the tree. I think it's a diary

and treasure chest of sorts."

They were all astounded and looked at the diary, like it was worth its weight in gold but decided to leave some excitement for the next day. They were a little bored, so they had a bike race (Sue won, Kyra was last, as always), played a little and decided to walk home.

"Hey, do you think the story is true?" Peter asked.

Sue said that it probably was since they found the well and the well is magical, this seemed to be anything they could talk about for the next ten minutes. So, they went to see the well for the last time and headed back home. By this time it was 5:30 in the evening, quite late as per Kyra's and Sue's parents. On the way home, Peter told Kyra, James and Sue to meet him in the forest the very next day and to bring the diary and chest with them so they can all see what is inside. All of them agree and head home, but the suspense of the book and chest is way too much!

CHAPTER 4

ADAM SMITH'S DIARY

The next day, Kyra woke up, brushed her teeth, got dressed, ate breakfast, grabbed the book and chest, woke James up, took her water bottle from her room and went down the stairs to ask her mom for permission to go and play. Her mother said, "Ok, but make sure you come back by sundown, don't go too deep in the woods, be safe. Oh, and do take James with you too, he's sleeping in his room."

So Kyra waited for James to wake up (which seemed like ages). Then both of them ran outside and met Peter, Sue and Sue's dog, Taffy.

"Hi! We're here," James announced.

"Everyone ready to see what's in the chest and book?" Kyra said and they all agreed excitedly.

They went to a silent, secluded spot in the woods and tried to open the chest, but it was locked, so they opened what they thought to be a diary. It belonged to a person called **Adam Smith**. In it was a sketch of the well, a beautiful woman and some notes of unknown plants and a very mysterious letter. It read……

Dear Adam,

Meet me at the well tonight at 8:00 and please bring the chest with you. I can't say how grateful and in debt I am to you for saving my sister Sierra the other day and any time you need anything or want help with something, remember, I'm there for you. You know what we must do, if something goes wrong, hide the chest and leave. Your diary too must be hidden till the well gives its location to the people destined to end the evil witch. You understand the witch is coming for us. Be safe and if you cannot make it to the well light a flare to let me know you're all right. Till then farewell....

Your faithful friend

Simon Anderson

They read the letter in a state of excitement and confusion. Peter said, "Who is this Adam Smith?"

Kyra noticed an introduction at the start of the diary. She read it out loud..........

I am Adam Smith; my life is dedicated to finding the Magic Well and eventually I found it with my 2 best friends **Simon Anderson** and his sister **Samantha Anderson. This well was created by my wife**. The well holds great power, only if you know how to control it and make it work for your benefit. Everything else is easy. You are most likely wondering who I am but that does not matter now. I am just a wizard of sorts and if you are able to read this you are a witch/wizard too, embrace your type of magic. Also, if you are reading this then that means I have already met my fate at the hands of the witch and need your help. If you wish to find me solve this riddle. Bring yourself to the trees in the town's middle find me, free me from my curse, before the witch gets any worse...

"Huh, anyone else fancy a riddle?" Peter asked jokingly.

"Are we really witches and wizards?" James asked, his eyes full of wonder, but alas! None of them really knew.

Kyra looked thoughtful while pondering upon the riddle. "Trees in the town's middle…I think it means the willow trees in front of the town hall …. but to bring ourselves there we must know his location," she spoke.

"True, I vote we go to the well and ask his location," Sue replied. Everyone agreed to Sue's idea. They walked back to the well.

At the well, James asked, "Well, could you tell us how to find Adam Smith? A riddle popped up on the stone. It read, ***Try to be courageous and brave, go then to the Ogre's cave. Leave a friend at the haunted shack, you will find the witch after that!***

James said excitedly, "It looks like now we have a mission!"

CHAPTER 5

PREPARING FOR A QUEST

Sue, Peter, Kyra and James asked their parents to go camping for a few days. As Kyra and James's parents were going out of town for a few weeks, they agreed on the condition Kyra keeps James safe. Sue's parents let her as she was old enough and because Sue's mother would accompany James and Kyra's parents, she did not think it was a bad idea. Peter's parents were all right with the idea too as he was always doing things of such sort but they told Peter that he could only go for two weeks and take some means of security like Sue's dog, Taffy (nothing went past Taffy's sense of smell!). The date they were planning to go on was just 2 days away! They packed water, lots of food, two tents, a lighter, some towels to dry themselves just in case it rained or they stop by a river, blankets, clothes, flashlights, matches if the flashlights stop working, jackets, sweaters, rope, a portable GPS, a guidebook, Peter's tinkering set, flares, umbrellas, shovel, dog food and treats (for Taffy) and first aid.

"We're all set!" Peter exclaimed. They had it planned out perfectly. Then they stayed over at Sue's, discussed the letter, played cards (of course, Kyra won, she was the smartest. Peter almost won and kept complaining that the game was rigged) and had dinner consisting of roasted chicken with boiled vegetables, ham, bacon, orange juice, pasta and home baked bread. It was as James described it, dinner big enough for a very hungry army. They talked for quite some time and Peter made another windup toy which looked disturbingly like Kyra.

"Bye, good night," they called out to each other as each of them went home.

Each one of the children was excited and ready to go for the quest. They were to go the next morning. That night everyone slept peacefully, that is, everyone but Sue. Sue kept rolling in her bed and couldn't help feeling that she was being watched by someone. She even opened her curtain, checked under her bed, in her closet, in the changing room, the big wooden cabinet, everywhere! But, nothing. No one was there, so she listened to peaceful music to help her fall asleep. But she was awake anyway, so she just played there, did some drawing and went for a walk in the garden (and jumped out of her skin when Taffy appeared behind her) too. After what seemed to be a thousand years, the sun came out. Sue got out of bed (and fell off it because she was sleepy but it's not like she slept anyway), brushed her teeth (and her hair), changed, took her backpack, ate breakfast and went to her mother Christine to say goodbye. "Be careful and take care of the others. I'll be away for two weeks, see you, darling. Don't do anything irresponsible or get in trouble, all the best! Be safe in the woods!" she said to Sue and embraced her.

Sue then left the house to meet her friends at the well in the forest, it was time for an exciting journey, to kill a witch!

CHAPTER 6

IN THE WOODS

Kyra, like Sue, was not having a great morning. James refused to wake up, they had not properly mended his bike and the chores were supposed to be done last minute, she was going to be late for sure. It was the first day of the quest. All the children were so excited that they woke up early on a holiday (a big thing for them they usually wake up by 10 o'clock on holidays)! They met in the woods at the well at 6:30 am. Sue and Peter reached first so they played with a small toy Peter made the previous night because he too did not sleep (what is up with that?), Kyra came a little later with her bags slung on her shoulder, looking tired, James was behind her yawning, looking like he just woke up with his messy, black hair.

"Sorry, I'm late. James just wouldn't wake up no matter how much I tried to get him to! So, I had to carry all the bags myself and that took forever and now I think that I bruised my left shoulder, thanks to him," Kyra said apologetically while glaring and staring daggers at James. Sue laughed and told Kyra it was all right as they all knew that James never woke up on time even on schooldays (and it seemed as though he was the only one to sleep the previous night). Sue then told the others about her sleeping problems and was surprised to know that both Kyra and Peter were also unable to sleep.

"It's probably just because you were too excited about the trip, that's all!" James said, looking distasteful.

Just then the stone in front of the well on which riddles appeared told them something. It said, **"Could you please pull the bucket up – The Magic Well"**

"Look, the well is telling us something!" James said, staring at the stone with his eyes wide (the last time that happened the situation was not good). The children did as the well told them. In the bucket was a map, in it was markings of the well, town, woods between, Ogre's cave, haunted house and an old shipwreck between Ogre's cave and haunted house.

"I wonder what that is," Sue asked, pointing at the shipwreck. They shrugged and said it might just be a landmark. After studying the map further, they decided to start riding their bikes because it was now 7 o'clock. Soon the children were deep in the forest. The air was cold and foggy as it had rained the night before. Peter handed everyone jackets "It's cold just the day we must be in the woods. It couldn't have been cold the day before yesterday or the day before that, it just had to be today!" he complained (he normally did that a lot when he woke up early on a holiday). They rode a long distance and after a while, they stopped at a fallen oak tree in the middle of the woods at around 1:35 for lunch and because James's bike was punctured again. Kyra lit a fire, cooked eggs, put some vegetables to boil in a pot and served lemonade. Sue collected everyone's jackets as by this time it was much too hot. Peter set their picnic mat and put the plates and spoons. Just then Taffy started growling, they checked the surroundings, but no one was there.

"She must've just seen a squirrel," Sue said, afraid but trying to reassure the others. I didn't miss anything, Taffy seemed to say.

"Oh, I'm stuffed and sleepy…. HAaaaw…. so slee ……
pyy," groaned James in the middle of yawning which set the
others yawning too (he had the biggest appetite compared to the
others even though he was the youngest and it was a wonder how
he was still short and lean after so much eating). After a big and
hearty lunch, they rested for a little while and fed Taffy. Peter and
James mended James's bike. Then they started walking with bikes
in hand again feeling quite full.

"Maybe we should ride again, it's much easier than going
on foot!" Kyra suggested but Sue had fallen off the bed last night
and hurt her foot a little, so the bumpy road was not that easy
on her. While walking, Peter looked at the sky, then at his watch
and said, "It's getting dark and late, and we're all tired. Let's set
up camp!"

CHAPTER 7

THE OGRE'S CAVE

They chose a spot near a stream and built the tents while James collected firewood and made the fire. The girls were to sleep in one tent while the boys were to sleep in the other one. After freshening up at the stream (of which water was as cold as ice), they got a flat stone, washed it and kept it on the fire and put slices of egg and bacon on it to be warmed. The moon was full and there were a few dangerous creatures in the woods but why should they be afraid? They had fire and almost everything they needed to scare away animals, and if there were any lurking around, Taffy would tell them!

"Can we have some apple juice?" Sue asked, a little thirsty. Kyra said yes and gave Sue a glass of juice.

"Do we have some more?" James asked eagerly (his face was burning because the others looked at him in awe as the food was so filling, there was no room for anything else)

"Yes, I brought some, I'll get them from the bag. Also, James if you eat so ravenously, we won't have food in five days because you ate three pieces of bread, two eggs, four slices of ham and three helpings of boiled vegetables!" replied Peter laughing.

After a light dinner(for everyone except James) and some scary stories, the children fell asleep. Taffy was awakened in the night and growled but none of the children awoke, so after she was convinced the intruder had gone further, she sat down, and she too fell asleep. In the morning, they brushed at the stream, changed clothes and packed the tents. By 7:30 am they were ready to go. Peter said enthusiastically, "According to the map, we are 20 minutes away from the Ogre's cave. It's a short distance, one and a half miles. Let's go!" When they reached where the Ogre's cave was supposed to be, there was just foliage and rocks.

"The map says it's supposed to be here," James said, looking confused.

Suddenly Taffy started barking loudly and ran behind some rocks. The children ran after her, their hearts beating quickly. There, hidden behind the rocks was the cave, the children cheered for Taffy and gave her a treat, Taffy herself seemed to strut as if she had done something truly heroic. From inside the cave, Peter could hear groaning. "I wonder what that is," he thought. There was only one way to find out, the children walked into the cave trying to tell themselves there was nothing to be afraid of (at one point James sneezed and all of them fell over in fright). It was too dark to see but that didn't matter, they had flashlights with them.

"Don't use all of them. We'll just use two for now. We have to save the battery," Peter said.

As the groaning became louder and louder, they could see a giant, green creature with blood streaming from its knee. It appeared to have red eyes because of crying. He bellowed, "I see you, puny kids. Go away, can't you see I do not want to be disturbed?"

Sue replied, "We mean no harm. We are here on a quest. If you like I could dress your wound, it looks painful, and I take classes in first aid."

The creature was astounded to receive such kindness. "In that case, please do. I am in such pain, but because you were kind to me, I shall tell you my tale!"

Long ago, like you, I was a human, but I was too brave. I had the courage to stand up against the bad witch after she had captured the good witch. I asked many people to join me, but alas! They were too scared. I fought her for a long time and lost miserably. I begged her for mercy and told her I have a wife and kids to take care of. She was furious and turned me into this hideous creature, made me her servant here, to do all the work for her. So, I have been, all these years!

CHAPTER 8

THE KIDNAPPING

Just as the story ended, the witch appeared, looking annoyed. She did not have green skin or warts, she looked like a regular lady, but she had the aura of evil and power. She looked at the kids and then at the Ogre while going into a rage. Then she said in a hoarse and rather frightening voice, "You dare meddle with my work, Ogre! Why are these stupid kids here? You! meddlesome kids know something you shouldn't. You are interfering in dark business and if you wish to live, leave my work alone. For this, I will punish you by taking him, goodbye!" Then she grabbed Peter by the arm and disappeared into a cloud of black smoke. As the smoke cleared, the children found themselves back at the well. Sue looked around hastily with tears forming in her eyes. From the well, something was emerging. Sue almost immediately recognized it as Taffy with butterfly wings and antennae.

"Oh, isn't she beautiful?" Kyra said, with her eyes full of wonder!"Yes, but we have to turn her back into a regular dog. Let's find someone who needs help," Sue said, holding back her tears. She wanted to get to the witch even faster now that she had Peter. But first things first, we must get back to the woods, she told herself. Kyra went to the market as she had to buy a new lighter and some food, James held Taffy and kept her from floating away while eating a sandwich (hey a kid needs a midday meal, right?) and Sue looked for someone who needed help.

Meanwhile, Peter was transported to a castle where the witch shoved him into a room and locked the door. He then realized he still had his flashlight and turned it on, the room had old supplies like a camera, broom and documents. Everything was covered in a thin sheet of dust. Peter tried walking but he had a searing, hot pain in his arm. When he pointed the torch at it, he saw that his skin was burned where the witch had touched him, but he had his water bottle and washed his arm to cool it down. Sue wandered across the roads for about 10 minutes before she came across an old woman who needed help crossing the road, after helping her she went back to James. Taffy had lost her wings and was back to normal, waiting for her mistress with her tail wagging. Sue hugged Taffy and gave her some food (flying does take up a lot of energy) and by that time Kyra was done shopping. James then said, "Ok back to the well then, I guess!"

CHAPTER 9

A NEW FRIEND

As they did, they were transported to an unknown part of the forest. "I'm hungry and tired and the sea is just there. Please, let's eat lunch!" James whined.

"Oh, all right. It does look fun!" Sue replied.

The children had loads of fun in the water and while eating, Taffy wouldn't spare a tidbit on the ground. After packing Sue thought she saw something in a bush. Probably a rabbit, she told herself (but then why was it so big?) but she found herself looking there every two minutes. They looked for places to set up camp. It would take more time now that Peter was not there. They decided to set up camp near the old shipwreck. Kyra looked like she was shocked, "This is the marking on the map. We are here for a reason!"

It made sense to the others. They were almost done when James gave a yelp. Behind them was a tigress and her cub. Sitting on the tigress was a young, masked figure about Sue's age. "Who are you and why are you here?" the figure asked.

"We mean absolutely no harm. We just need to find out why this ship is on our map," Sue replied. The figure went through their stuff and then through the diary.

She looked suspiciously at each of them and said, "I'll let you stay here. On one condition, you take me on your quest! And if you betray me, I'll set the tigers on you."

When they asked why she wanted to join them she said that nothing ever happened in this part of the woods and that she was keen on adventure. The children agreed. The figure removed its mask. It was a beautiful girl about Sue's age with light freckles, dark brown hair and light green eyes. There was a necklace with a key on her neck. James thought she looked familiar to him like he had seen her somewhere, but he just couldn't remember. The girl said, "I'm Carmen. What are your names?" The children quickly introduced themselves. "I have lived in this wreck almost my whole life. I never thought I would have the company of humans in this part of the woods," she said smiling. James was scared out of his skin as the tiger cub approached him. "That is Scarlett, she is my best friend. Her mother's name is Shakira."

Kyra gave Scarlett a pet, she nuzzled up to Kyra affectionately. Taffy, meanwhile, was trying to figure out how cats could be so big. They all had a wonderful dinner as Carmen had hens, cows and tigers as pets. The children finished dinner and went to sleep after a great deal of chatting. Deep in the night, Carmen was awoken by the sound of Scarlett, Shakira and Taffy growling.

CHAPTER 10

AN ENCOUNTER AT NIGHT

"Wake up, Sue! Hurry, someone's there! Come on, wake up," Carmen whispered sharply in Sue's ear. Sue immediately woke up to the sound of Carmen's voice; someone was there!

They could make out shadows of two people. Next thing they knew, Taffy pounced on the figure and Scarlett joined soon after. There was a series of shouting, barking and growling followed by a loud thud and the sound of footsteps running away. Sue was getting scared, what if the men hurt Taffy and Scarlett? She couldn't just call a vet! Oh, she hoped the people didn't hurt them. Carmen lit a lamp and they saw Taffy and Scarlett coming toward them quite all right and not harmed at all. Sue was overjoyed. "Good girls!" she called to them as she took out a packet of dog treats. Surprisingly Scarlett liked them though she wasn't a dog. Suddenly Carmen noticed something in Taffy's mouth, it was a something like a book.-.

"Sue, I think I know who we saw. We have their diary!" Carmen told Sue. They quickly woke the others.

CHAPTER 11

OFF WE GO!

The children opened the diary at around 11:30 pm.

"Anyone getting tired of diaries yet? 'Cause I sure am!" James exclaimed. In the diary there were pictures; a picture of Sue in her bedroom 3 days ago when she felt she was being watched, one where the children (Carmen excluded, they hadn't met her yet) were standing at the well, one of Sue sleeping with Kyra in a tent and a similar one with James and Peter, also one of Carmen.

"Hey this is from the night before when I thought I heard voices!" exclaimed Carmen.

James's face lost colour. "I think we are being followed!" he said.

This made them scared, but they were three tigers one dog and four people against two. They could overpower them if they wanted to, but the feeling of being followed was frightening. The children agreed to leave for the haunted house the next day and fell asleep again with the disturbing thought of being followed. The next morning was bright and cheerful, everyone helped in packing their supplies. Turns out carmen had lots of useful stuff in her shipwreck. They all took a bath and splashed around in the water of the sea. Then they changed clothes and were to be off on their way but just then James sprained his ankle. "Oh, no! We can't go, James cannot walk," sobbed Kyra.

"Who said anything about walking?" Carmen said with a sly grin and whistled, out of the shadows, Scarlett, Shakira and Shakira's sister Sasha, another tiger, emerged. Carmen mounted Shakira and told James to sit behind her whereas Kyra and Sue sat on Sasha. Scarlett and Taffy ran behind them contentedly playing with each other. While on their way, the children discussed the topic of the haunted house.

"The riddle said we have to leave someone there!" said James. He had a disturbing thought that he was scared to leave his sister but also knew that he would not be much help fighting the witch whereas Kyra, Sue and Carmen were older and would do a better job than he could. After walking for a while, they sat down for breakfast consisting of cold ham sandwiches, marmalade, canned peaches and lemonade along with biscuits and bones for each of the pets (if you can call tigers that).

"The best breakfast I ever tasted," Sue said.

All of them were a little surprised at how less James had eaten this morning, but they let the matter be. After some time, they sat down for a break.

"According to the map we should walk for half a mile more, we should be able to see the haunted house," Kyra said.

"Great, I'm already tired, so half a mile won't hurt, also can someone pass me some lemonade or water? I'm sweating a lot," James said.

"If you finish the lemonade in one day, what will we drink? I really think you are eating too much!" Kyra replied jokingly as she passed him the lemonade.

"Let's go quick, the sun will set in 4 hours at best. We have to be done with leaving someone and setting up camp by then," Carmen warned the others (she had an old watch so they could now know the actual time).

CHAPTER 12

THE HAUNTED HOUSE

They started walking and could soon see an old house which was practically falling apart. There were two livable rooms and one bathroom, but the kitchen had fallen in and the roof of the hall was not there anymore. They walked inside and Carmen swore that she heard someone weeping but decided not to tell the others. Unexpectedly James said with tears in his eyes, "I should stay. I can't fight the witch, rescue Peter or find Adam Smith. This mission needs me to stay. You should go, I'll be fine." This came as a shock to the others.

Kyra hugged her brother. "It's very brave for you to do so, but I promised mother I would keep you safe. I should stay."

James smiled, "I told you I will be fine, plus what's the worst that could happen?" he said, forcing himself not to cry again.

Kyra gave him a bag with water, food, first-aid, clothes and a tent, she also left Sasha with James, just in case. "Well, we best be off but the riddle said we should find her after leaving you, but we didn't," Kyra said thoughtfully.

Suddenly the map grew and had a new endpoint. "Look!" Carmen pointed at the map. "I bet that is where the witch is!"

They said goodbye to each other. "All right, we best be on our way! Goodbye James, be safe!" Sue called as they began walking and left James behind.

After a short while, they found a place to set up camp. "Let's set up some traps in case we're being watched," Kyra suggested.

"Good idea, Kyra. I'll put up the tents. Carmen, you can make the fire and get the food ready, and Kyra will set the traps!" Sue said, full of enthusiasm.

Meanwhile, James had already used the bathroom, made a fire and set up his tent, now he was ravenously eating a large salad (boy he could work up an appetite).

Kyra made a trip-line triggering a bucket of water and a couple of bells so they could hear if someone is approched. She also told Taffy and Scarlett to sit in front of the tents so they could be on guard.

"Nothing could be safer!" Carmen exclaimed.

They too had dinner of noodles and salad. Then they explained to Carmen what happened to Peter. At last, Carmen went to her tent and Sue and Kyra to theirs. The children fell asleep, not to be disturbed....

CHAPTER 13

FINDING THE WITCH

The next morning, the girls woke to see none of the traps had gone off. At first, they thought nothing of it! But soon it dawned on them.

"Maybe they thought we were still at the haunted house with James!" Carmen said.

"I bet you are right because they have been following us for some time. Why would they just stop? They must have something to do with the witch," Kyra replied.

"It makes sense. Let's change and pack. We better get moving quickly if we want to reach the witch and rescue this friend of yours," Carmen suggested. They packed the food and tent and changed with incredible speed.

"That better be a world record!" Sue exclaimed and all of them giggled.

"It sure is good having friends who can talk. Usually, at this time, I eat berries with Scarlett and the others," Carmen sighed. While on their way, Taffy started barking furiously. Even Scarlett was growling furiously while Shakira stood in front of them and roared to scare off the intruders. At this point all of them were scared. Sasha was with James to keep him safe, but Shakira roared once more. It was loud and terrifying.

"We're being followed. The weird people we saw yesterday caught up with us, be quiet," Kyra said as they hid. They could hear footsteps, so they decided they have to hide. Carmen hid in a small cave with a bush to cover the entrance. She took the pets with her too; Sue was inside a huge bush and Kyra was up a tree.

CHAPTER 14

CAUGHT

The footsteps got louder as they saw too-small figures, they looked like garden gnomes except five times bigger.

"I thought the kids were supposed to be here," one of them said in a gruff voice.

"I heard them. They are here, I tell you. I can smell that dog of theirs. Don't worry, the witch will reward us handsomely if we bring the meddlesome brats!" said the second figure.

"We know you're here somewhere, children. Come out. Come out wherever you are, come on. We don't have all day, come out," they said.

The spot where she was hiding was dusty so Kyra was developing an uncontrollable need to sneeze slowly, she healed it till she could hold it no more and loudly sneezed, "Ayacuchoooooooooooo!" She then felt something or someone grabbing her ankles and hitting her head before passing out.

By this time both Sue and Carmen were panicked. "We know the rest of you are there now!" The gnome creatures spoke. Carmen silently slid to the back of the cave, trying not to be seen. After seeing Kyra being grabbed and put into a bag, Taffy could not restrain from the urge to bark. This is how even Carmen was caught. "Ah! Let me go! Let me go, I tell you. Ah! Help!" she called before the creatures gagged her and stuffed her in a sack. Sue now panicked and decided to be very quiet as the figures looked for her when they gave up. She decided to follow them!

CHAPTER 15

BEING RESCUED

The gnomes (their names are Bo and Flo as Sue heard) walked for a long time, but at last, they sat down to set up camp. Now Sue had Taffy, Scarlett and Shakira with her so she could get her friends back with ease, but her plan was to follow the gnomes to the witch's lair and find out their plan. Although Sue had the upper hand she decided to set up camp at a distance and not make a fire too big. Sue slept alone that night wondering whether she could save the mission on her own. Sure, she had done plenty of things on her own but saving the whole mission? That was a tough thing to do, so she slept. At around 5:45 in the morning, she woke up early, packed, changed, fed the pets and was ready before the gnomes. She followed them (at a safe distance, of course) for what seemed like ages. Finally, at around 4 o'clock in the afternoon, they came to what looked like a huge, black mansion with its own personal thunderstorm above it. Everywhere else was bright and sunny, but this part had a thunderstorm. Odd.

At the gates, Flo said, "Let us in, by the power of the evil witch!"

Huh, what an easy password, mine (which is Sue 'n' Taffs 1 2 3) is much better, Sue thought laughing to herself (because everyone joked that her password was too easy). After they were in, she quietly said the password and went in, the plants near the big, black, iron gate were none like she'd ever seen but, on the inside, there were a few plants which she had seen as drawings in Adam Smith's diary. There were also several odd inscriptions on the wall, like a spell to keep the mansion safe. The gnomes had tossed Carmen and Kyra in a dark room and latched it from the outside before leaving for lunch. Sue, quietly and discreetly, lifted the latch and woke her friends up.

CHAPTER 16

LET'S FIND OUR FRIENDS!

Kyra and Carmen were tied up and gagged, waiting to be rescued, so when Sue came in, they weren't surprised, just happy.

"Where are we?" Carmen asked, looking around.

"Oops, sorry. I forgot you were in the sack. We're in the witch's secret lair," Sue said, full of excitement. She then opened her bag and gave Kyra and Carmen some ham sandwiches.

"Thanks for the food, we were starving! But shouldn't we look for Peter?" Kyra asked with concern in her eyes.

"You are absolutely right. Let's find our friends!" Sue said, with enthusiasm.

They walked down a long corridor and could hear the witch scolding someone. She said, "Keep quiet and stop crying or I will feed you to my wolves! You are soon to be released if you behave properly. Your meddlesome friends have caused too much trouble as it is! But I will have my revenge. I will if it's the last thing I do. Now your friends are in another room. They have another girl with them. You must ask her for the key on her neck and I will be able to open the chest containing the only thing that can kill me. We will see your friend shortly at 5:30 pm. Till then you will have time to think if you rather perish with them or live on and never utter a word about this!" Saying so she disappeared in a cloud of smoke.

CHAPTER 17

AN EXCITING DISCOVERY

"Carmen, why was she talking about your necklace? Is it important?" Kyra asked, looking at Carmen. After all, they didn't know her for very long. What if she was also an enemy?

"I don't know, I've had it since I was born. My father gave it to me. I still have his picture, too, look!" saying so Carmen opened and thrusted a folded picture of Adam Smith to the others!

"Carmen, Adam Smith, the man we are looking for is your father! This means you're a witch and only you can defeat her," Sue exclaimed in utter disbelief.

"You mean, he is alive! He must have given the necklace to me knowing that you would come to me!" Carmen said, overjoyed with tears rolling down the sides of her face.

"Ooh, I think you're right and the key fits in the chest and whatever is inside can defeat the witch! Come on. Let's go tell Peter," said Carmen.

As they swarmed inside, Peter's eyes grew wide. He started asking all sorts of questions. "How did you find me? Who is she? Where is James? Why do you have two enormous tigers with you? Ugg, I'm so confused!"

The children laughed and told him everything that happened since he was kidnapped. Peter was happy that his friends were safe and he was introduced to Carmen, but mostly he was just shocked.

Sue said, "Let's find Adam Smith! Oh, and by the way, he's Carmen's father."

Peter (who said that they could have told him earlier that Adam is Carmen's dad) told them that the only thing that could defeat the witch was in the chest that Carmen's key can open.

"Where is the chest?" Kyra asked concerningly.

"That is the tricky part. You see, the witch has cast an enchantment that will not allow us to touch the chest and the only way to break it is to utter the witch's real name, which we don't know," Peter said dejectedly.

Sue tilted her head and said, "Then let's find out her name!"

CHAPTER 18

THE WITCH'S NAME

Ha, that sounds like the story of Rumpelstiltskin! Sue chuckled after that. Kyra just then had the brilliant idea to look for anything with a name on it, a document, prize, drawing, certificate or a diary, anything with a name! But disappointingly they found nothing (just my luck, Kyra thought). Peter was just about to give up hope when something caught his eye. It seems as though Carmen saw it too. It was an old, dusty picture of the witch holding a certificate of magic on the last shelf.

"Guys, quick! Look at the certificate, it must have her name on it!" Peter told the others.

The certificate read –

This is to certify Ms. <u>Wendy</u> witch as a qualified trainee in magic. We are proud to have taught you at this school and are happy for your success. We congratulate you on all your success and wish you a happy future in your career in magic.

– Lilac School of Magic

"Wendy, that's her name. Wendy! Wendy Wendy… Wendy!" Kyra squealed in delight.

Carmen stood in front of the chest and said, "Wendy, Wendy, Wendy!"

Surprisingly, nothing happened. A confused Sue gently touched the chest. This was the moment of truth, what was going to happen? She was all right! Carmen took her necklace off and fit it in the keyhole. What was going to happen next?

CHAPTER 19

WHAT'S IN THE CHEST?

The chest opened with a soft click as Carmen felt anxious. For a minute the children were stunned by the blinding light. Inside the chest was a ruby, chiseled in the shape of a knife (A ruby is a type of red diamond). It was sharp enough to stab someone.

"I think Carmen should keep it, after all, she is Adam Smith's daughter!" Kyra suggested.

As soon as Carmen held the blade, they heard the witch's servants Bo and Flo advancing toward them. They all said in unison, "RUN!"

The children panicked. Carmen hid (again with the pets) in a large cabinet, Sue was behind a bookshelf and Kyra was under a blanket on top of the cabinet Carmen was in. Peter sat where he was always seen. Bo comes in with a plate of food. He looks around suspiciously and hands the plate over to Peter, looks around again and walks out slamming the door behind him. After confirming that the coast is clear, Peter tells his friends to come out, he mentions to them that the witch wants to meet them at 5:30.

Kyra then worriedly exclaimed, "Get up, Peter! We must hurry and get out of here and find Adam Smith!"

CHAPTER 20

ADAM SMITH

They walked along the corridor until they reached the end. There was a room with a lock. The lock was open but enchanted.

"Wait a minute!" Carmen said as she fit the knife into the lock.

Peter suggested that the knife can overpower the witch's magic. They walked into the room and saw a figure sleeping, Carmen held the knife up to see as it glowed red. Down on the floor was Adam Smith! He smiled weakly and said "My daughter, Carmen. I see you possess the object to destroy the witch but first, you must tell me how I have been found!"

After a great deal of talking, Carmen told her father to tell her how to kill the witch, his reply was to get near enough and stab her right through her heart. Peter shuddered at the thought. Kyra looked at the clock, it was 5:15! They carefully planned. They would go to the rooms they were in and when the witch comes in Sue would stab her with the knife while Taffy, Scarlett and Shakira take care of Bo and Flo. But the plan didn't work as planned…

CHAPTER 21

A MARVELOUS PLAN

The children scrambled to their positions while Sue hid, she had locked Bo and Flo in a room with Taffy, Scarlett and Shakira and tied their limbs. If they dare to move it was at their own risk. As they had planned, the witch came into the room with Peter dragged behind her and told them to sign a contract (A paper saying agreeing to do or give something). Kyra could not stand seeing Peter being treated so badly and hurled herself toward the witch, but she just swatted Kyra away like a leaf in a gust of wind. Carmen ran toward Kyra but the witch said to focus and if Carmen did not pay attention she would fling Kyra off the balcony. So Carmen took the contract, it said:

Do you Carmen Smith, offspring of Adam Smith and Sierra Anderson, the good Witches/Wizards, agree on willing terms (or forceful, it doesn't really matter) to give me the chest that is rightfully mine along with the key? In case you don't, I shall see that you are sent to the realm of monsters. If you wish that you, your family, home and your friends be left alone you must also agree to have your memory wiped off this whole incident of magic. Think about it. It's only a one-time offer.

Yours Truly the Bad Witch

Sign here _______

Carmen slowly almost handed her the key and said in a flash, "Now!"

Sue stabbed with all her might, fearing that it would not reach her heart. Everything started to explode and shake, like it was an earthquake. Eventually, they thought they had done something wrong that it had not reached her heart, or it did not work properly because the witch was too powerful. But at last, the witch shone like a supernova and disappeared.

CHAPTER 22

THE GOOD WITCH

The children were still stunned when Adam walked over to them. His eyes had bags around them and his cheeks were sunken, but he still looked happy because why wouldn't he be? He'd just been reunited with his daughter after 12 years! Carmen ran to help Kyra and soon she was all right though she now had a large cut on her forehead which Sue tended to. They were talking but behind them a part of the wall opened up, revealing a beautiful woman in a blue dress. Although she looked starved, her aura made all of them feel like they had just drunk three cups of coffee, taken a shower and woken up from a nap, that is, it made them feel happy and energized.

"Sierra! I thought you were dead! What happened?" Adam said with tears of joy.

The woman who was the good witch said that the bad witch Wendy kept her and took her power. But now that the bad witch was gone, she has her powers back! She then introduced herself to the children as Carmen's mother and Adam's wife, the good witch Sierra.

The children gasped. "Does that mean Carmen is a witch too?" Kyra asked.

Turned out Kyra was right. Carmen was a witch! (Or at least a jr. witch)

CHAPTER 23

BACK HOME AT LAST!

Sierra snapped her fingers and James appeared with his supplies and Sasha. They had a happy reunion and lots of talking while Sue fetched Scarlett, Taffy and Shakira. Sierra hugged Shakira and said thank you for taking care of Carmen and returned her to her true form in which Shakira has transparent skin reflecting all the colors of the rainbow and was much bigger in size. She can also breathe fire and ice (which James thought was totally awesome!). The children were amazed and asked to be sent home, they were immediately engulfed in smoke as they found themselves at the well. Beside the well was a beautiful cottage with blue roses on the roof and an enormous garden.

"This is where I live, if Carmen wishes to stay with us, I shall be overjoyed. If not, I understand," Sierra said.

Carmen immediately hugged her and agreed. The children headed toward their houses bidding each other farewell until next time!

www.ingramcontent.com/pod-product-compliance
Lightning Source LLC
LaVergne TN
LVHW041758190726
843493LV00008B/2682